Lilly's Lost Lunch

The Sound of L

by Joanne Meier and Cecilia Minden • illustrated by Bob Ostrom

The Child's World®

Published by The Child's World®
1980 Lookout Drive
Mankato, MN 56003-1705
800-599-READ
www.childsworld.com

The Child's World®: Mary Berendes, Publishing Director
The Design Lab: Design and page production

Library of Congress Cataloging-in-Publication Data
Meier, Joanne D.
  Lilly's lost lunch : the sound of l / by Joanne Meier and
Cecilia Minden ; illustrated by Bob Ostrom.
     p. cm.
  ISBN 978-1-60253-408-7 (library bound : alk. paper)
  1. English language—Consonants—Juvenile literature.
2. English language—Phonetics—Juvenile literature 3.
Reading—Phonetic method—Juvenile literature. I. Minden,
Cecilia. II. Ostrom, Bob. III. Title.
  PE1159.M459 2010
  [E]—dc22   2010002921

Printed in the United States of America in Mankato, MN.
July 2010
F11538

NOTE TO PARENTS AND EDUCATORS:

The Child's World® has created this series with the goal of exposing children to engaging stories and illustrations that assist in phonics development. The books in the series will help children learn the relationships between the letters of written language and the individual sounds of spoken language. This contact helps children learn to use these relationships to read and write words.

The books in this series follow a similar format. An introductory page, to be read by an adult, introduces the child to the phonics feature, or sound, that will be highlighted in the book. Read this page to the child, stressing the phonic feature. Help the student learn how to form the sound with her mouth. The story and engaging illustrations follow the introduction. At the end of the story, word lists categorize the feature words into their phonic elements.

Each book in this series has been carefully written to meet specific readability requirements. Close attention has been paid to elements such as word count, sentence length, and vocabulary. Readability formulas measure the ease with which the text can be read and understood. Each book in this series has been analyzed using the Spache readability formula.

Reading research suggests that systematic phonics instruction can greatly improve students' word recognition, spelling, and comprehension skills. This series assists in the teaching of phonics by providing students with important opportunities to apply their knowledge of phonics as they read words, sentences, and text.

This is the letter l.

In this book, you will read words that have the l sound as in: *late, left, lost,* and *lunch*.

It is a busy morning
at Lilly's house.

Lilly wakes up late.

She does not like to get up.

Her left shoe is lost.

She has to look a long time.

"Lilly, time for breakfast!
It's getting cold. Let's go!"
says Dad.

Lilly doesn't listen. She likes to play with her dog Lucky.

"Lilly, let's go! We will be late for school."

Oh no! Lilly's lunch is lost.

Where could it be?

Lilly and her dad look and look.

"Where did you see it last?" asks Dad.

It was on the little table.

Oh look! Lucky likes

lunch, too.

Fun Facts

It is easy to hear a door slam or a bell ring, but it is harder to listen to other noises. When a doctor wants to listen to your heart or lungs, she needs to use a special instrument called a *stethoscope*. Some people don't like listening to loud noises or might have a hard time falling asleep if there is noise around them. These people often buy earplugs so they don't have to listen to sounds they don't want to hear.

You have probably heard that breakfast is the most important meal of the day, but you need to eat lunch and dinner, too! In 2003, the president proclaimed one week each year to be National School Lunch Week. During this week, which always begins on the second Sunday in October, kids have a chance to learn about nutrition and eating healthly.

Activity

Planning a Healthy Lunch for Your Friends

National School Lunch Week is in October, but you should practice healthy eating habits every day. Talk to your parents about inviting your friends to a party at your house where only healthy foods will be served for lunch. Instead of chips, offer vegetables. For a main course, consider making sandwiches with whole wheat bread and a lean meat such as turkey. You can serve yogurt and fresh fruit for dessert.

To Learn More

Books
About the Sound of L
Moncure, Jane Belk. *My "l" Sound Box®*. Mankato, MN: The Child's World,
2009.

About Listening
Binkow, Howard, and Susan F. Cornelison (illustrator). *Howard B. Wiggle-
bottom Learns to Listen*. Minneapolis, MN: Thunderbolt Publishing, 2006.
Meiners, Cheri J., and Meredith Johnson. *Listen and Learn*. Minneapolis, MN:
Free Spirit Publishing, 2003.

About Lunch
Kelley, True. *School Lunch*. New York: Holiday House, 2005.
Norfolk, Bobby, Sherry Norfolk, and Baird Hoffmire (illustrator). *Anansi Goes
to Lunch*. Atlanta, GA: August House Story Cove, 2007.
Palatini, Margie, and Howard Fine (illustrator). *Zak's Lunch*. New York:
Clarion Books, 2004.

Web Sites
Visit our home page for lots of links about the Sound of L:
childsworld.com/links

Note to Parents, Teachers, and Librarians: We routinely check our Web links to make
sure they're safe, active sites—so encourage your readers to check them out!

L Feature Words

Proper Names
Lilly
Lucky

**Feature Words in
Initial Position**
last
late
left
let's
like
listen
little
long
look
lost
lunch

About the Authors

Joanne Meier, PhD, has worked as an elementary school teacher, university professor, and researcher. She earned her BA in early childhood education from the University of South Carolina, and her MEd and PhD in education from the University of Virginia. She currently works as a literacy consultant for schools and private organizations. Joanne lives in Virginia with her husband Eric, daughters Kella and Erin, two cats, and a gerbil.

Cecilia Minden, PhD, is the former director of the Language and Literacy Program at the Harvard Graduate School of Education. She is now a reading consultant for school and library publications. She earned her PhD in reading education from the University of Virginia. Cecilia and her husband, Dave Cupp, live outside Chapel Hill, North Carolina. They enjoy sharing their love of reading with their grandchildren, Chelsea and Qadir.

About the Illustrator

Bob Ostrom has been illustrating children's books for nearly twenty years. A graduate of the New England School of Art & Design at Suffolk University, Bob has worked for such companies as Disney, Nickelodeon, and Cartoon Network. He lives in North Carolina with his wife Melissa and three children, Will, Charlie, and Mae.